Sisi
and the cassowary

Arone Raymond Meeks

A Scholastic Press
book
from
Scholastic Australia

Long ago, when the world was new,
a girl called Sisi lived with her tribe
in a rainforest close to an ocean reef.
Every morning she and her mothers and
her sisters went inland to the waterfall
to bathe and refresh themselves for
the day.

Sisi and her sisters slipped from the bank and away from the watchful eyes of their mothers. There was a sandbar on the far side of the waterhole. Sisi could see a long-necked tortoise bathing on a log in the sun.

'Let's see if we can catch the tortoise,' Sisi said.

But her sisters were too busy diving and splashing in the cool water.

Sisi took a deep breath and dived under. She saw fish and snakes and eels. When she surfaced, she saw something large floating in the water.

'That must be a log,' she thought, but suddenly it swished a long tail.

It was a crocodile! Sisi dived and swam away as fast as she could.

She reached the water's edge with her lungs bursting for air and her arms aching.

As Sisi pulled herself onto the bank, she noticed that her sisters and mothers had disappeared.

'Coo-ee!' she shouted. 'Where are you?'

There was no reply.

'Coo-ee!' she shouted again, but all she could hear was the calling of birds and the sound of wind rustling through the canopy above.

Sisi walked along the banks looking for the spot where she and her sisters had been playing. But everything looked different—the trees, the rocks, even the waterfall.

Sisi realised she was lost.

'What would my mothers do?' Sisi asked herself. 'I know! They would light a fire to make smoke.'

She remembered how her father had taught her to gather dry paper-bark and two dry sticks, and she began to make a fire. She twirled one stick into the other and blew on them until they became hot. First a curl of smoke appeared, then a few sparks and, at last, a tiny flame. Sisi placed some fine twigs on top to make a blaze.

'This smoke should attract someone's attention,' she thought as she waited.

Suddenly a small, bright blue berry hit Sisi on the head. As she reached to pick it up, a boy sprang from the bushes and grabbed it.

'Who are you?' Sisi asked, 'and why did you do that?'

'I live here,' the boy replied. 'My name is Bindi. I know many of the fruit trees in the forest, and these are my berries.'

'Then maybe you know the way to the waterfall,' said Sisi. 'I've been separated from my family and I am lost.'

'I could help you,' said Bindi. 'But my father sent me to gather berries and if I don't find enough before nightfall I won't be able to return home.'

'If you show me the way,' said Sisi, 'I will help you gather enough fruit. If we work together we will both get back to our families before night.'

The boy agreed and Sisi made a basket out of bark. Together they wandered along the riverbanks collecting bright blue berries until the sun had touched the edge of the rainforest canopy.

'We should start back,' said Sisi as she gathered a last handful. 'My mothers will be worried.'

But when she turned to the boy, he had disappeared.

'Coo-ee!' she shouted. 'Coo-ee! Is anybody there?'

There was no reply.

It was almost dark. Sisi was lost and far from home, and Bindi had let her down.

Suddenly a huge blue and purple bird strutted from the bush. Sisi jumped back as it started towards her. But when she looked into its eyes, she thought she saw someone she recognised.

'Could it be?' she wondered, remembering Bindi's dark eyes.

The bird put its long neck against Sisi, nudging her to climb astride its back. Then they set off through the forest. Sisi clung to the bird's dark feathers as it strode through dense vegetation and crossed countless streams. Under its powerful, clawed feet the path was blue with berries.

After some time, Sisi heard the sound of splashing water. They had reached the waterfall at last! The bird stopped, stretching its long neck down to peck at the berries. Sisi slid from its back and reached to gather some berries too.

When she looked up again, the bird had run away into the bush.

Sisi heard someone calling her. It was her mother, searching for Sisi by the banks of the waterhole. They ran to each other, and Sisi began to tell about the boy, the berries and the bird.

'I will show you the bird's footprints,' Sisi said.

But when she looked, all she could see were the footprints of a boy.

Her mother lifted Sisi onto her shoulders and headed back to the campsite by the reef. On the way, Sisi's mother told the story of the cassowary, and of how it knew its way through the forest because of the quandong tree and its bright blue berries.

Dedicated to my mums

Shirley, Pauline, Colleen and Valerie

ARM

Scholastic Press
345 Pacific Highway
Lindfield NSW 2070
an imprint of Scholastic Australia Pty Limited (ABN 11 000 614 577)
PO Box 579
Gosford NSW 2250
www.scholastic.com.au

Part of the Scholastic Group
● Sydney ● Auckland ● New York ● Toronto ● London
● Mexico City ● New Delhi ● Hong Kong ● Buenos Aires

First published in 2002.
Copyright © Arone Raymond Meeks, 2002

Reprinted in 2004 and 2005

National Library of Australia Cataloguing-in-Publication entry

Meeks, Arone Raymond
Sisi and the cassowary

For primary school students.
ISBN 1 86504 525 X (pbk).

I. Title.

A823.3

Typeset and designed by Design on the Side
Typeset in Goudy and Pepita

Printed in Singapore by Imago

10 9 8 7 6 5 4 3   5 / 0